To our hippy-hoppy grandkids—Theo, Archer, Claire, Luke, Kaitlyn,
Logan, Evan, Maria, Moriah, Alexandria, Rockey, and Brandon

Thank you to Annie, Kirsten, and my critique groups
for helping to bring a teeny-tiny toad to young readers. —P.A.

To Hector and Virgile —A.W.

Visit us on the Web! rhcbooks.com
Educators and librarians, for a variety of teaching tools, visit us at RHTeachersLibrarians.com

Library of Congress Cataloging-in-Publication Data is available upon request.
ISBN 978-0-399-55676-0 (trade)
ISBN 978-0-399-55677-7 (glb)
ISBN 978-0-399-55678-4 (ebook)

The text of this book is set in ParmaTypewriterPro.

The illustrations were rendered in watercolor and China Ink.

Book design by Rachael Cole

MANUFACTURED IN CHINA
2 4 6 8 10 9 7 5 3 1
First Edition

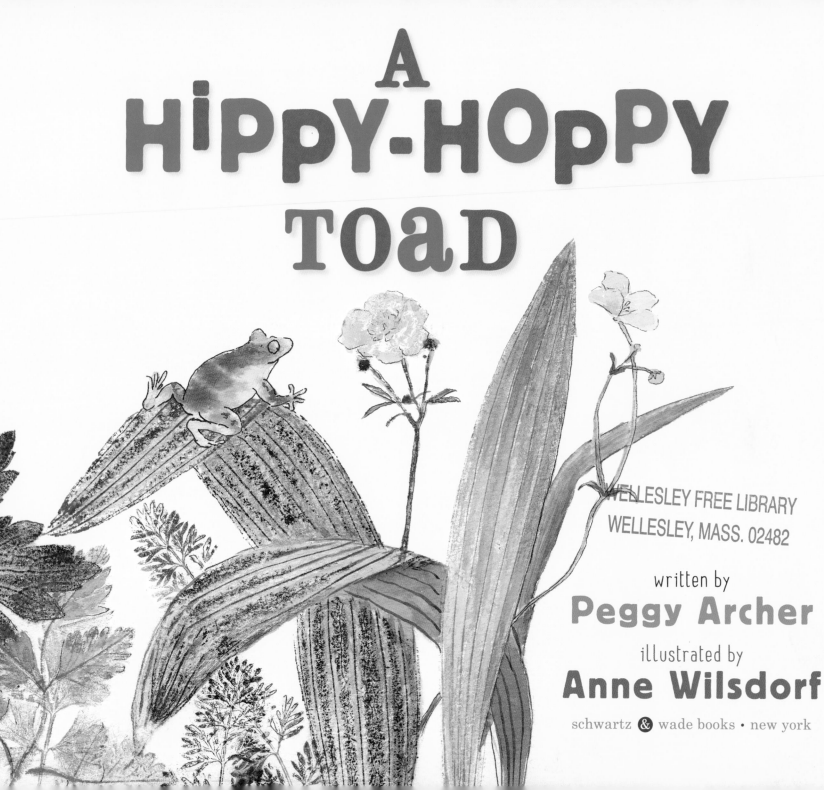

A HiPPY-HOPPY
TOAD

written by
Peggy Archer

illustrated by
Anne Wilsdorf

schwartz & wade books · new york

In the middle of a puddle
in the middle of a road
on a teeter-totter twig
sat a teeny-tiny toad.

Snap! went the twig.

Up! went the toad.

And he landed on a tree
by the side of the road.

On the raggy-shaggy tree

by the side of the road

on the rough, gruff bark

sat the teeny-tiny toad.

Peck!

went a bird.

Jump! went the toad.

And he tumbled to a flower

in the park by the road.

On a fuzzy yellow flower
in the hush-rush breeze
sat the teeny-tiny toad
in the shadow of the trees.

Buzz! went a bee.

Hop!

went the toad.

And he jumped to the grass
at the side of the road.

In the slippy-sloppy grass

where the toad sat still

was a happy-snappy cricket

with a singsong trill.

Chirp!

went the cricket.

Treeeee! went the toad.

And he chased the chirpy cricket

to the gravel down the road.

In the stony, gritty gravel
in the shade by the road
in the calm, quiet morning
sat the hippy-hoppy toad.

Woof! went a dog.

Then he hopped to the top
of a stone by the road.

On the fat, flat stone
in the warm, still air
lay a tough-scruff lizard
with a sharp, steady stare.

Slink! went the lizard.

Blink!

went the toad.

And he hip-hop-plopped
to the dry, dusty road.

Down the dry, dusty road
where the toad crept along
under bunchy, crunchy leaves
came an easy, breezy song.

Whoosh!
went the wind.

Swoosh! went the toad.

And he flew to a leaf

hanging close to the road.

Round the flippy-floppy leaf

came a whirlwind gust

of a huff-puff wind

with a cloud of dust.

Bump! went a shoe.

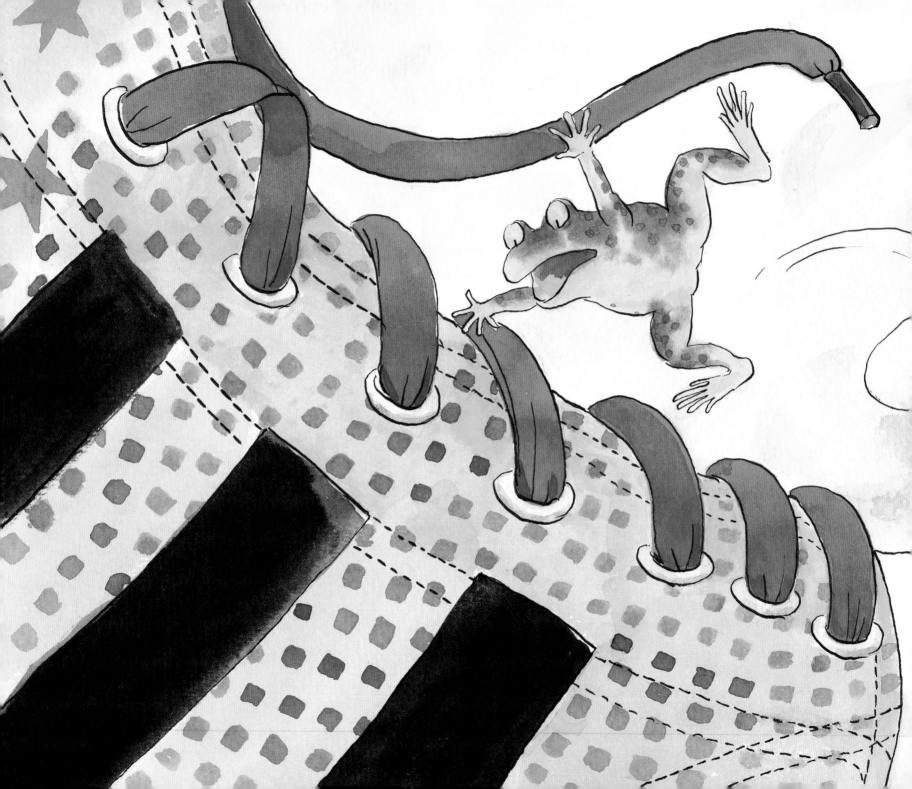

Thump! went the toad.

And he landed on the sneaker

as it ran down the road. . . .

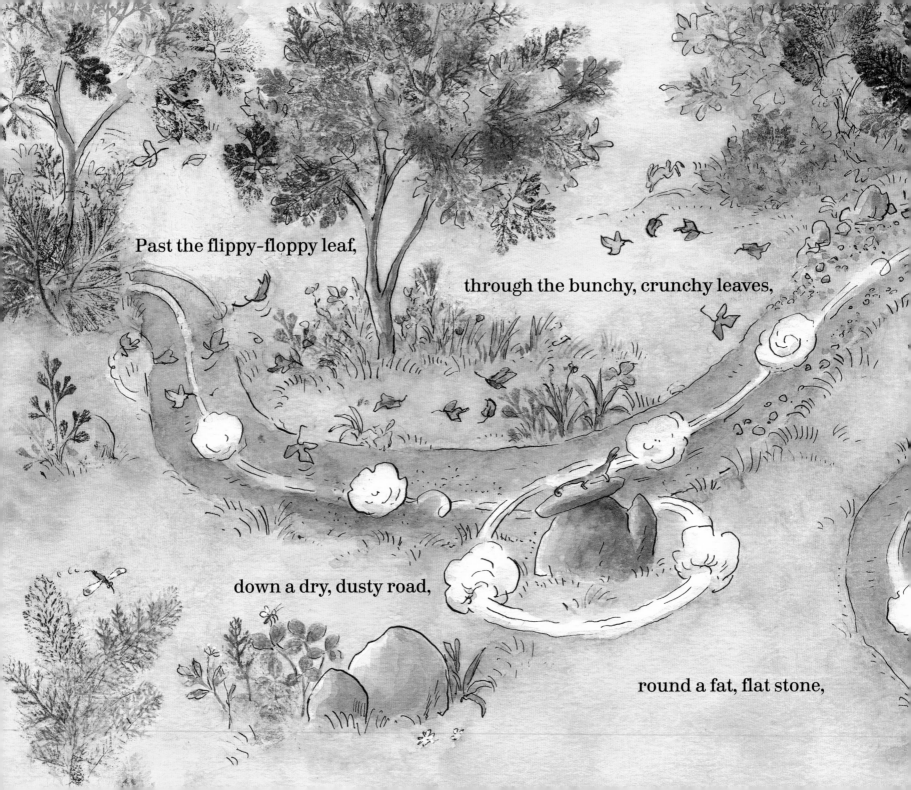

Past the flippy-floppy leaf,

through the bunchy, crunchy leaves,

down a dry, dusty road,

round a fat, flat stone,

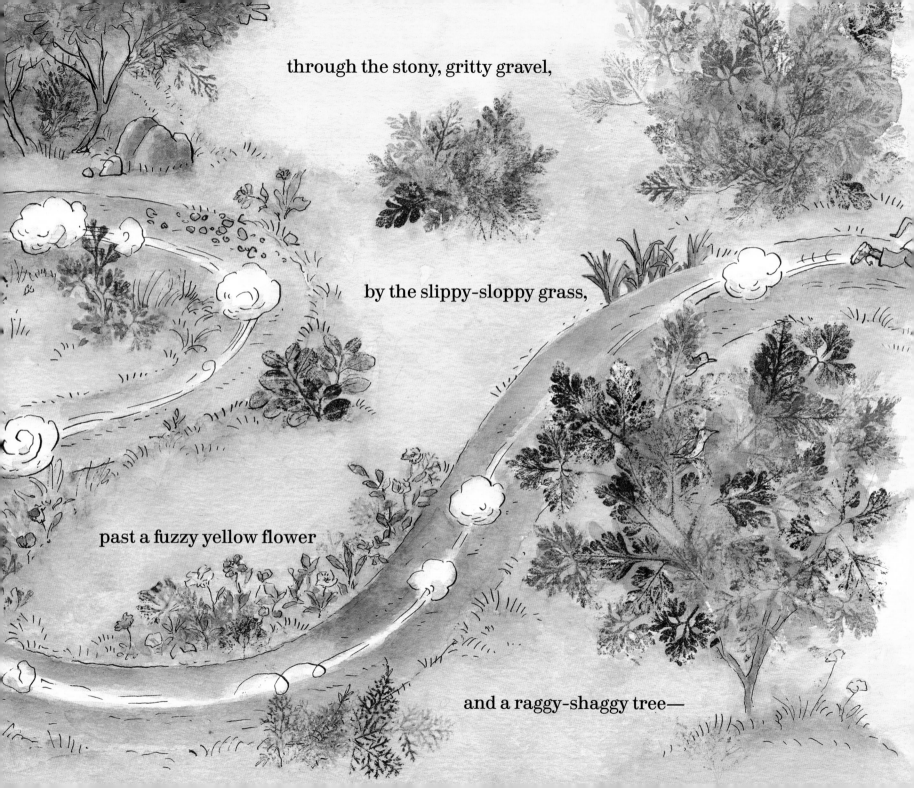

through the stony, gritty gravel,

by the slippy-sloppy grass,

past a fuzzy yellow flower

and a raggy-shaggy tree—

went the bump-thump sneaker
with the teeny-tiny toad
hanging on for the ride
as they raced down the road.

The shoe went **zag!**

The toad went **zig!**

And he sailed through the air

to a teeter-totter twig.

In the middle of a puddle
in the middle of a road
on a teeter-totter twig
sat a teeny-tiny toad....